For Herschel Silverman, jazz poet
and Bobby McFerrin, scat man
and to the memory of Miles Davis
and John Coltrane
          —Jonathan London

To my nephew Peter,
my uncle Emmett,
and to Layne, my muse.
          —Woodleigh Hubbard

Text © 1993 Jonathan London
Illustrations © 1993 Woodleigh Marx
     Hubbard
Art direction by Karen Pike.
Type design by Laura Lovett.
Printed in Hong Kong.

Library of Congress Cataloging-in-
     Publication Data
London, Jonathan, 1947-
Hip Cat/written by Jonathan London;
     illustrated by Woodleigh Hubbard.
p. cm.
Summary: Hip Cat journeys to the city by the bay
     to live his dream of being a jazz musician.
ISBN:0-8118-1489-0 (pb) ISBN:0-8118-0315-5 (hc)
[1.Cats–Fiction. 2. Musicians–Fiction.] I. Hubbard,
Woodleigh, ill. II. Title.
PZ7.L8432Hi   1993
[E]–dc20   93-1179
CIP AC

Distributed in Canada by Raincoast Books
8680 Cambie Street, Vancouver, B.C. V6P 6M9

10 9 8 7 6 5 4

Chronicle Books
85 Second Street
San Francisco, California 94105

Website: www.chronbooks.com

Acknowledgments

To Victoria, Kendra, Jill, Molly, Karen, Laura and
Vickie T. I am blessed to be working with you—a team
full of moxie, talent, creativity and wit.   —W. H.

Hip CaT

by Jonathan London

illustrated by

Woodleigh Hubbard

chronicle books

San Francisco

He was a hip cat
  a hep cat
  a cool cat

living all alone in a riverside shack:
Oobie-do John the Sax Man Scat Man,
   the cool cat man.

One day he said to himself,
"All I want to do is to make jazzzzzy music."
So he picked up his sax—
what his friends called his "ax"—
and tipped his beret and said,

   "Scat, cat. *Go, cat, go!*
  Hip Cat daddy-o's got a horn to blow!"

  And
     that
       cat
         scat.

He hopped on the night train—
the faster-than-light train—
and in no time he came
    to a city by a bay.

    It was a bebop-
        rebop city,
    a bongo-congo roller-coaster-jazz-in-your-bones city.

Hip Cat moseyed along,
  singing a song
    swinging his sax.

He slipped into MiNNie'S CaN Do on Fillmore and said,
  "Sweet Minnie, I want to blow my horn!"

Big Max the Manx cat was reading poetry at the mike,
stomping the floor to the rhythm of his words.

And when he was through,
    our hip cat hero with a horn to blow BLEW.

His sax bobbed
　　　and swung, screeched
　　　　　and
　　　　　skonked, purred
　　　　　　and
　　　　　　barked.

The cats in the club said, "*Go, cat, go!*"
And Hip Cat wailed into that horn.

　　　He wailed his song of longing,
　　　　his song of joy,
　　　　　　his song of loneliness and looniness—

and the crowd went cRaZy.

The joint was jumping.

Toes tapping
and cats bopping.
Chairs dancing
and shadows hopping.

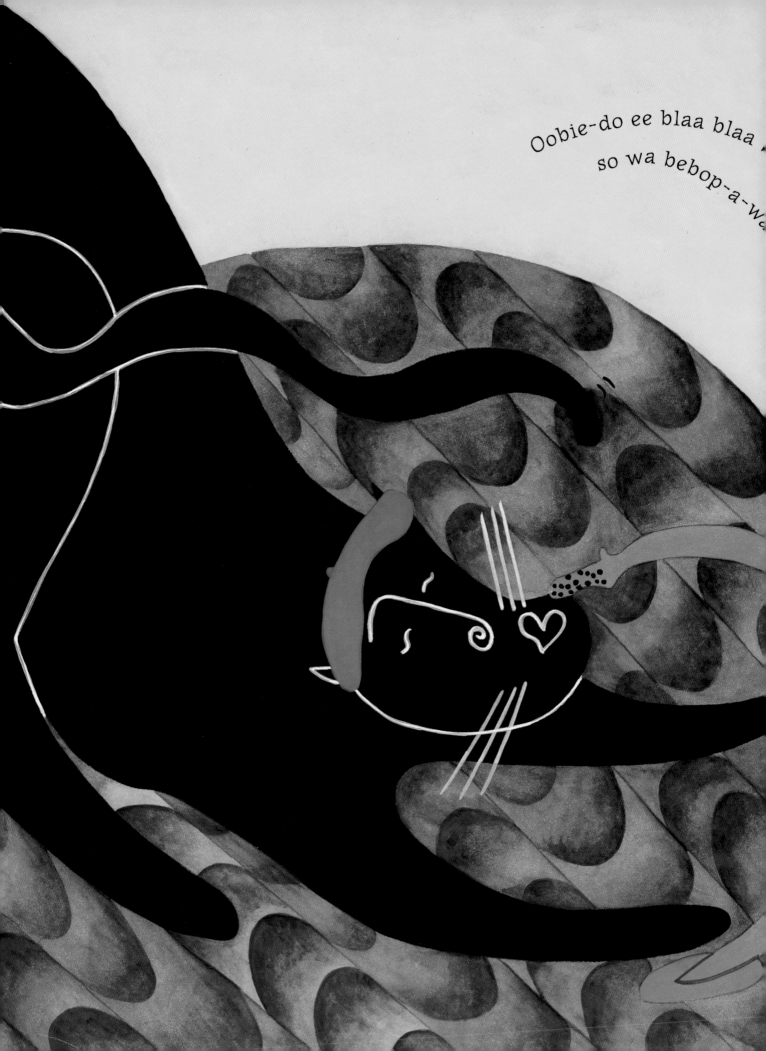

Oobie-do ee blaa blaa
so wa bebop-a-wa

Still tapping his toes and bobbing his head,
Hip Cat stopped blowing and started oobie-doing instead.

oobie wa-ditty, my cat is a kitty

His new fans loved him and Minnie hugged him.

ng bang blam

He was a bad cat
a mad cat
a rad cat.

But Minnie could only pay him with peanuts.
Now he was a penniless hip cat daddy-o
with a tail to tell and a tale to wail.

He hit all the jazz joints in town,
     looking for a gig
          that would pay the rent.
He was getting tired of living in a tent.

But the joints were owned by the top dogs.
     If cats wanted to make it
          they couldn't fake it.

          He said,
     "If dogs can run free,
          why not me?"

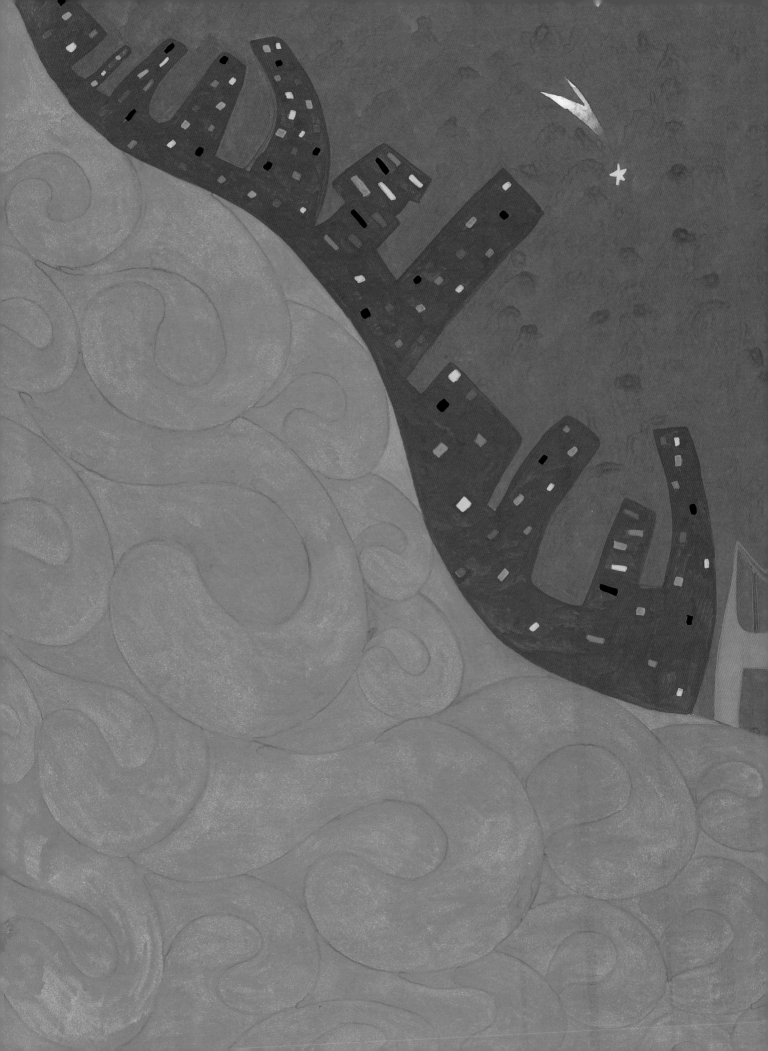

So Oobie-do played his sax under the bridges.
He played in the fog
and he played on the ridges.

He played all day
and he played all night.
He played for no pay
but he kept up the fight.

But he had to eat, and there was no money in sight.
So he played his sax at all the tourist traps.
Tourists with cameras tossed coins in his cap.
Then he became a short-order cook
        at the Doggie Diner.

        But he knew
        he could do
something
        a *whole* lot finer.

One night, he slipped back into MiNNie's CaN Do.

Minnie said,
    "Oobie-do, how do you do?"
Oobie-do said,
    "I'm feeling kind of blue."

Minnie said, "Sing it. You can do."

Big Max and some minx cats and cats in minks
were jamming on their axes, playing some licks.

They said, "Who's that cat, the cat from the sticks?"
Then they remembered, and shouted, "Oobie-do!
Do what you do, let the cats out of the zoo!"

So he blew his horn
all bluesy and forlorn.
Then he started singing better than ever,
    remembering the river
    where he was born:

Oobie-do ee blaa blaa blaaa

so wa bebop-a-wamma bing bang blam shoobie wa ditty, my cat is a

Then Oobie-do blew everybody away with his horn.

And pretty soon word got around.
Even the top dogs paid top dollar
for Oobie-do to wail at all the clubs.

He played in the hungry i.
He played in the Hungry You.
He played in the Purple Onion

and when he was·through . . .

... the crowds went hog wild.

Now wherever he went he went in style.
He tore down his tent and paid the rent.
He ate tall ice creams and paid all his bills.

They called him a jazz magician,
     a great musician,
          and a poet of the blues.

And when he rode the cable cars over the hills,
his feet flew out in his shiny new shoes.

     Oobie-do shouted,

"Do what you love to do,
          and do it well!"

He was a hip cat daddy-o with a tale to tell.
He told it with his music
    and his oobie-do wa-ditty-wa shoobie-wa-day.
      My cat is a kitty and we play all day.

Even the fat cats
and the river rats
    back home
    listened to his music on the radio.

They called him,

    "One cool daddy-o."

He was
      a hip cat
      a hep cat
      a cool cat
a bad
mad
rad cat

Oobie-do John the Sax Man Scat Man

      the long
      sleek
      cat man.